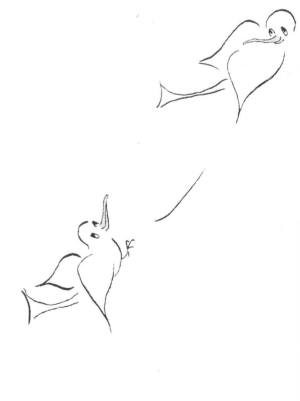

Originally published in France as *Le Merle Blanc*
by Editions Duculot, 1987. PRENTICE-HALL
BOOKS FOR YOUNG READERS is a trademark
of Simon & Schuster Inc.

Translated by Jennifer A. Otlet
Cover design by Meredith Dunham
Printed and bound by Bietlot, Belgium
10 9 8 7 6 5 4 3 2 1

Library of Congress Cataloging-in-Publication
Data. Weck, Claudia de, 1953–   13 Happy
Street. Translation of: Le merle blanc.
Summary: A little girl's search for her lost bird
takes her to an unusual house where she learns
an important lesson about friendship. [1.
Friendship—Fiction.   2. Birds—Fiction]
I. Lager, Claude.   II. Title.   III. Title: Thirteen
Happy Street. PZ7.W41255Aaf   1988   [E]
87-7160   ISBN 0-13-918434-1

13
HAPPY STREET

CLAUDIA DE WECK

Text by Claude Lager

PRENTICE HALL BOOKS FOR YOUNG READERS
A Division of Simon & Schuster Inc.
New York

Fanny had a rare white song bird that
she kept in a cage.
She called the bird Blanche.
But Blanche was bored. She dreamed of
stretching her wings and flying free.

One day, finding the cage door unlatched, she
hopped out and flew away.
Fanny burst into tears; Blanche was her
dearest friend.

"Come back, Blanche! Come back!" she cried.
But Blanche took no notice.

Fanny followed Blanche as she flew
across town.

"Stop! Please get back in your cage !"
begged Fanny.

Finally, Blanche came to rest on the
branch of a tree.
Safely out of reach, she began to sing.
She's just teasing me, thought Fanny,
and rang the bell of number 13 Happy Street.

A snowman came to the gate.
"My white bird has flown into your garden.
Have you seen her?" asked Fanny.
"No," answered the snowman, "but she might be
in the house. Come in and look around."

Fanny stepped inside.
"I'm looking for my little white bird. She's
escaped from her cage."
"We haven't seen anything" said the monkeys.
"Come and play with us instead."

But Fanny didn't want to play.
She looked in the kitchen.
"My little bird – is she in here?"
"No, she isn't," said the girl, "but would
you like a cup of hot chocolate?"

Fanny opened another door.
"I've lost my white bird – have you seen her?"
"A white bird? Certainly not! Why don't you
sit down and eat something?"

But Fanny wasn't hungry.
She asked Mr. Pig, who was lying on a sofa.
He suggested she look in the "Lost and Found"
columns of the newspaper.

Then, at last, Fanny spotted Blanche.
She was sitting on the banister, singing.
But as Fanny approached she hopped away
again and disappeared.

Fanny looked into another room, where a
man was playing the piano.
"Hello, little girl. Would you like to
hear me play?" he asked.
"I haven't got time now," replied Fanny.

Suddenly Blanche swooped by, right under
Fanny's nose.
"This is too much!" exclaimed Fanny.
"*Why* won't you get back into your cage?"

Blanche flew into the bathroom.

"Now what are you doing?" asked Fanny.

"Do you think I can't see you?"

Fanny followed Blanche into the bedroom,
where the little bird was peeping over
the top of a big bunk bed.
"What are you doing up there? I can help
you down if you're frightened."

But Blanche simply spread her wings and
flew away.
"Oh, wait for me, I'm your friend!" cried
Fanny as she tried to catch up with the
little bird.

Now where is she, wondered Fanny.
Perhaps she just doesn't like me anymore.

Fanny stopped and thought for a long time.
The little bird did seem much happier
than she'd been before . . . .

"Blanche, Blanche! I know what you want!
Just wait and see!"

Fanny picked up the cage
and threw it away.

Now Blanche knew
that Fanny understood.

For Fanny had learned that even the most
beautiful cage in the world could not make
Blanche happy if she wasn't free.

And if you want to keep your friends you
must never lock them up.

Fanny and Blanche said goodbye to everyone
at number 13 Happy Street.

Blanche knew that she was free to soar in the sky and sing in the trees, and Fanny knew that Blanche would always come back home.